Roger's War

Robert Swindells

Illustrated by Kim Palmer

mammoth

For Bob and Joan Honey:
Fans when I had no fans
R.S.

For Phoebe
K.P.

First published in Great Britain in 1999
by Mammoth, an imprint of Egmont Children's Books Limited
239 Kensington High Street, London, W8 6SA

Text copyright © 1999 Robert Swindells
Illustrations copyright © 1999 Kim Palmer

The moral rights of the author and illustrator have been asserted

The rights of Robert Swindells and Kim Palmer to be identified as
the author and illustrator of this work have been asserted by them
in accordance with the Copyright, Designs and Patents Act 1988

ISBN 0 7497 3749 2

10 9 8 7 6 5 4 3 2 1

A CIP catalogue record for this book
is available from the British Library

Printed in Great Britain by Cox & Wyman Ltd,
Reading, Berkshire

Contents

One

War changes everything. I know I'm not the cleverest kid in the world but I have noticed that. There's a song they play on the wireless. An American song, 'Johnny Got a Zero', and it shows how war changes things. It's about this kid in America, Johnny, who's no good at school. When they have tests he gets a zero, which means no marks. He's a bit like me, that Johnny. The other kids laugh at him, same as me. They follow him home singing, 'Johnny got a zero, Johnny got a zero, Johnny got a zero today.' He's the town dunce.

Then the war comes, and Johnny joins the airforce. The American Airforce. He gets to be a fighter pilot, fighting the Japanese. The Japanese have a really good fighter plane called the Zero, and you've probably guessed what happens. Yes, Johnny turns out to be such a wizard pilot that he's shooting down Zeros all over the Pacific, and everybody's singing, 'Johnny got a Zero, Johnny got a Zero, Johnny got a Zero today.' My mum says it's rubbish because they don't let dunces be pilots, but I don't care. It's my favourite song.

The war's changed Picton as well.

Picton's our village, and I used to know everybody who lived here. They were all *born* here. If somebody spotted a stranger in Picton it was all around the village in no time.

Then, when I was nine, the war came and my dad went off to be a soldier. A lot of the other dads went as well, and strangers started appearing. Workmen. Land-girls. Pilots. The pilots lived at Picton Hill where the aeroplanes are. British fighters then, American bombers now because the Americans are in the war.

That changed things around here as well. Americans in the village. For one thing, they can get all the sweets they want. No rationing, and us kids can get them too if we know what to do. What you have to do is, go up to some Americans and say, 'Got any gum, chum?' It makes 'em laugh 'cause they think we talk funny, but then they open their pockets and out come chocolate,

Lifesavers, chewing-gum: more sweets than they've got down Fenner's shop. Americans call it candy whether it's chocolate or whatever it is, but we're not bothered what they call it. It's sweets, and the war can go on for ever and we won't mind as long as the Americans don't leave Picton.

My big sister feels the same, but not because of candy. Her name's Wendy, she's seventeen and she's dotty about Americans. She goes out with them. Dancing. Mum doesn't like it, mind. She shouts at her sometimes. 'You wouldn't behave like this if your dad was at home, young woman.' She says Americans can't be trusted not to hurt English girls, but that's daft because they're on our side. Anyway, Wendy's nearly grown up so she takes no notice.

Now and then she'll bring a boyfriend home to tea. Americans are *really* polite, they call Mum *Ma'am*, and they nearly

always bring tinned peaches or a tin of ham: stuff they can get easily and we'd queue all day for if it was in the shops, which it isn't. Mum reckons not to like Americans, but you don't see her refusing the ham and peaches, or the stockings some of 'em give her.

That's a story in itself, women's stockings. You can't get 'em 'cause they're made of silk and ships aren't bringing silk from China any more. They're too busy bringing food, so Wendy and her friends paint their legs.

You probably think I'm fibbing but I'm not. There's this horrible pinkish-brown goo they buy at the chemist, that's supposed to look like silk stockings when you daub it on your legs. It doesn't really, but they kid themselves it does. The daftest bit is, they have to paint a thin dark line down the back of each leg to look like a seam. Now this seam has to be dead straight or it doesn't look right, so a girl can't do it herself. She has to get her mother to do it, or a friend. Once, Mum wouldn't do Wendy's seam because she was off out with a man Mum didn't like the sound of, and Wendy was so desperate she asked me. I tried, but I kept giggling because I could see up her frock, and in the end she fetched me a terrific smack across the ear and told me to bugger off. If Mum had heard her she'd never have got out of the house again.

Anyway, that's why it's a special occasion when some American produces a pair of stockings.

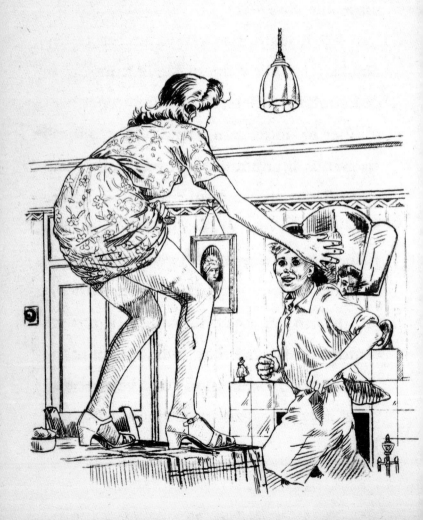

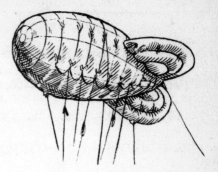

Two

What I really want to tell you about is how *I* got in the war.

I've always wanted to be in it but it's not easy if you're a kid. I mean, you can go round collecting salvage and if you're a girl you can knit socks for sailors, but they won't let you join the army. I know because this boy at school, Frank Littlejohn, once told me kids can join the Infantry. He said that's why it's *called* the Infantry, so I went along and volunteered and a big sergeant chased me down the street. Well *I* didn't know. Frank Littlejohn's clever, see, and I'm not. Mum said he ought to be ashamed of himself.

I'm in the war now though, because of something that happened a few weeks ago. I'm going to tell you all about it, only first you've got to know what a barrage balloon is.

A barrage balloon is grey, it's as big as a house and it's filled with gas. The gas makes it float up into the sky but it can't fly away

because it's on the end of a long steel cable that's fastened to the ground. Sometimes this cable is half a mile long, so the balloon'll be half a mile up. They're not round, barrage balloons. They're long, like extra-fat sausages, and they've got three stubby fins at one end, a bit like a bomb.

The RAF has hundreds of them. They stop enemy bombers making low-level attacks because if a low-flying aeroplane hits a balloon cable, its wing falls off and it crashes.

They put barrage balloons round important targets such as docks and factories and goods' yards on the railway. Their cables make a sort of fence in the sky.

Now you know about barrage balloons I can get on with the story. I'm Roger, by the way. Roger Fallowfield.

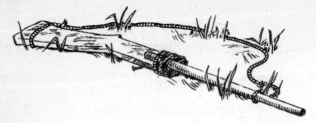

Three

It was autumn 1942 and I was twelve. It was a Saturday and I was playing at soldiers in Picton Woods. I was by myself as usual, so nobody was being the Germans. I had to *pretend* there were Germans, but that was better than playing with Ginger Kitteridge and Clive Simcox and them, because they always made *me* be the Germans.

In this game I was a British commando, operating behind enemy lines. I was so busy throttling sentries, laying explosive charges and keeping the Germans at bay with my Sten gun that I lost track of time and, before I knew it, it was nearly dark.

My mum doesn't like me to be out after dark because of the blackout. She thinks I might get shot by the Home Guard. Sounds silly because the Home Guard are on our side, only there was this kid last winter, a deaf kid on a bike, in the dark. This wasn't Picton, it was somewhere else. Anyway, this kid liked to watch the planes at an aircraft factory, and one night when he was cycling near this factory the Home Guard shot him dead. They're always on the lookout for spies, and they must've thought he was one. They shouted to him to halt but he was deaf and couldn't hear 'em so *bang*! that was the end of him.

Mum tells me this story and I says to her, 'But *I*'m not deaf, Mum,' and she says, 'You're not *deaf*, lovey, but you've got to admit you're a little bit *daft*.'

I hate being called daft. Especially by Mum.

Anyway it was nearly dark and Picton was half a mile away so I started hurrying across the fields. The sky in front of me was streaked with orange, and suddenly I saw a great black shape there. It looked like a whale, or a flying elephant. I was scared stiff. The grown-ups are always whispering about secret weapons and I was sure this was one, coming to get me.

It was approaching with no sound, which made it more terrible somehow. I was about to turn and run when I noticed the cable. It was just a thin black line down the sky, but one end was attached to the object drifting towards me and I recognised it. It was a balloon cable. I was looking at an escaped barrage balloon.

They do escape sometimes. In a high wind. I knew that, and I knew something else as well. They're dangerous, especially to aeroplanes and especially at night.

Think about it. You're flying along in the dark and a loose balloon's drifting

across your path, trailing its cable. You
can't see it. First thing you know is when
you hit it and then it's too late. You've lost
a wing or propeller. You can bale out if
you're high enough but the plane's a
write-off. One less for the enemy to worry
about.

And they're dangerous in other ways too. That steel cable is heavy. Half a mile of it might weigh a ton or more and, if the balloon's flying low like this one was, it can trail across buildings, knocking off chimneypots and tiles. It can smash windows and even kill people who get in its way, and it might bring down power lines, leaving whole towns without electricity.

In daylight there'd probably have been a whole lot of people running after this balloon, but in the dark nobody knew where it was. Nobody except me.

I didn't stop to think. If I had, I'd have thought, *uh-oh, here comes a steel cable to cut me in two*, and I'd have dodged it and run away. I didn't do that. What I did was, I waited till the balloon dragged its cable through the hedge into my field, then grabbed it. Not the end. The end was still somewhere over in the next field. I just lifted a section and sort of looped it over my arm.

It was a lot thicker than I'd expected, and much heavier. Luckily there wasn't much wind so it wasn't moving fast, otherwise I might have lost my arm. As it was, I could feel the rough-plaited wires

scraping the skin off through the sleeve of my shirt. It stung like mad and I nearly let go, but then I thought, *what if a commando was bothered about a bit of skin? He'd never get the job done, would he?* I gritted my teeth and hung on, and the balloon started dragging me across the field. I thought I'd be able to stop it – hold it on the cable like somebody flying a kite, but I was wrong. I found myself running, even though the balloon seemed to be drifting slowly. I could see the hedge I'd squeezed through a minute ago. In a few seconds I was going to crash into it and then the cable would be torn from my grasp, and I might end up with a stiff branch through my stomach.

I had to think fast, which isn't easy for a dunce. Luckily for me, two elm trees stood in this field, close together, their branches merging high up. I swerved and staggered towards them, letting the cable run over my arm as the balloon pulled on it, praying there was enough slack so I could reach the trees before it ran out.

There was. I lugged my burden round and between the two old trunks in a figure-of-eight and the cable was still snaking through the grass with no end in sight, so I did it again. As I completed this second manoeuvre there was a rasping, creaking noise. The loops tightened round the trees as the drifting balloon took up the slack. The cable slipped up the trunks, flaying off strips of bark to expose the white flesh underneath. I wondered fleetingly whether the trees felt the sting of this as I did in my arm, which probably shows how dim I am.

The cable creaked but slipped no further and the elms were too sturdy to budge. Up there, invisible now in the darkness, the rogue balloon strained like a dog at the leash, but it's journey was over. I'd captured it. Roger Fallowfield had done something right at last.

Four

I let the cable drop and it was then I really felt the pain. It was so bad I felt sick and had to lean against a tree. It was too dark to see anything, but I felt my sleeve and found it wet from wrist to shoulder. As soon as the sickness passed I set off again, one arm hanging. The orange had gone from the sky. Stars twinkled. I must get home. Must get home.

You should've heard Mum when I staggered in. You probably *did*. Mind you, I was putting it on a bit, the wounded-

hero act. Well, it's not every day you get the chance, is it?

'It's only a scratch,' I said as she and Wendy gaped at my arm. I got that out of a Douglas Fairbanks film, but then I went and spoiled it by yelling at the top of my voice all the time Mum was bathing it. Douglas Fairbanks winced,

I remember. Once.

This bathing and bandaging didn't start the second I appeared, by the way. As soon as I told Mum about the balloon, she ran next door to use Mrs Pearson's phone. When she'd gone, Wendy said, '*I* saw that film too. "Only a scratch." Douglas Fairbanks was wounded by a rapier, not a flipping *balloon*. Only a duffer like you could go and get himself hurt by a balloon, so you can keep the hero stuff for Mum: it won't wash with *me*.'

Mum phoned the police, told Sergeant Clough her son had left a barrage balloon fastened to the elms in Crowtrees Field. The Americans were due back any

minute from a daylight raid on Germany. They had to be warned not to fly too low over Crowtrees when circling to land. Only when she'd seen to this did Mum turn into Florence Nightingale.

I was given Ovaltine and put to bed, which Douglas Fairbanks wasn't in the film. Actually, I didn't mind. It gave me chance to relive my moment of glory, and to imagine what the kids would say tomorrow when they found out what I'd done. They wouldn't laugh at me *this* time, that much was certain.

I fell asleep in the middle of a fantasy in which I was given the VC and made Head Boy at school.

Five

When I woke up next morning my arm
felt as if it was on fire. It throbbed and
burned inside Mum's neat bandage,
which was splotched with red in one or
two places. My back hurt like
mad when I sat up, and I
couldn't bend or stretch to
dress myself. I managed
to put on my dressing-
gown and hobble
downstairs, feeling
every inch the

wounded hero. Funny how you can even enjoy pain when you know everybody's about to make a fuss of you.

It wasn't like that at all. I limped into the kitchen ready to be modest when the hero-worship began, but Mum gazed at me solemnly and Wendy looked at the floor.

'What's up?' I murmured.

'Roger,' said Mum, putting her arm round my shoulders, steering me to my chair. 'Something's happened. Something sad, but it's not your fault. You mustn't think you're to blame, because everybody knows you're not.'

'What?' I rested my sore arm on the table and looked up at her. 'Have I done

something bad, Mum?'
Dread seeped like ice-
water into my bones.
Was it *Dad*? Had she
had a telegram? But
then why would she
say it's not *my* fault?

She sighed, shaking
her head. 'No dear, you
didn't do anything wrong, but
the balloon . . . the balloon brought down
an American plane.'

'What?' I couldn't believe what I was
hearing. An American plane? 'But you
phoned the police, Mum. You *told* them.
Didn't they warn the bombers?' My voice
broke up. I started to cry as Roger the

hero crumbled, leaving Roger the dunce.

She stroked my hair. 'It wasn't one of the bombers, darling, it was a fighter. One of the escort fighters from another base. It was just one of those things . . . it can't be helped.'

'Oh, Mum, why did you *have* me when I never do *anything* right?' I opened my mouth and howled my despair, tears scalding my cheeks. 'I'm useless. *Useless.*'

She held my head, pressed my face into her pinny, stroked my hair. I flung my good arm round her waist and clung on, convulsed with sobs. Today had promised to be so different. So different. I hadn't cared about the pain. It was going to be *worth* the pain to become a new Roger. A Roger who didn't knock things over every time he moved. A Roger people didn't laugh at. Now all that had dissolved, leaving only the pain.

She held me till I cried myself out, then mopped my face and made me drink some milk. I couldn't eat anything. 'My arm hurts,' I mumbled. 'I'm going back to bed.' Even *I* couldn't help the enemy if I was in bed.

I lay in the semi-darkness, hoping to die. How could I possibly show my face at school tomorrow? Face my so-called chums? My teachers. The kid who kills Yanks. *Hey, Roger, it says here Hitler's sending you an Iron Cross.* The new Roger. Hah!

The only good thing was Wendy. I told you she's dotty about Americans, and I thought she'd hate me now that I'd killed one. She didn't. She came and sat on my bed and held my

hand and said, 'Don't blame yourself, Kiddo.' Kiddo was an expression she'd picked up from one of her boyfriends. 'What you did was not only brave: it was clever. Not many people would've thought of wrapping the cable round those trees. You really *are* a hero, and the rest is just bad luck.'

It didn't make me feel much better at the time but all the same, it was nice of her.

As it happens I needn't have worried about school. Not for a while anyway, because as the day wore on I developed a fever. My arm had become infected. It was so bad by tea-time that Mum made Wendy run for the doctor. I don't remember anything about the next few days. Mum says I kept slipping in and out of consciousness and it was touch and go whether I recovered or not.

Six

When the fever finally broke, everything had changed again. I couldn't take it in at first – it seemed like a continuation of the weird dreams you get with fever. I opened my eyes and Mum was sitting in the chair beside my bed. She smiled. 'How are you feeling this morning, dear?'

'Hungry,' I mumbled. My memory was sort of fogged over but I knew vaguely that there was something nasty waiting to be faced.

Mum nodded. 'Good. Breakfast's on its

way.' She smiled again. 'You're quite the hero, you know. People are waiting to meet you. Important people.'

It was coming back to me about the balloon. The American fighter. I looked at her. 'What d'you mean, hero? Is it a joke, Mum?'

She shook her head. 'No joke, Roger. Remember the plane? The one that hit your balloon?'

'Course I remember, how could I ever forget? It was American.'

She nodded. 'That's right. An American fighter, *with a German pilot.*'

It was true. Seems a Mustang fighter crash-landed in France a year ago and the Germans patched it up, got it flying. They left its American markings on, and one of their pilots started joining the swarms of Mustangs which escort

American bombers to and from their targets. In the heat of battle nobody noticed one extra fighter. He'd fly back to England with the bombers, and when they were circling their base with their wheels down, flying really slowly, he'd open fire on one of them. Its crew wouldn't have a chance – they'd have relaxed because they were practically home, and their plane would be too low to recover. It would crash, killing everybody on board, and the German would streak away at treetop-level to avoid interception. He'd done this time after time over various bases, with the American Airforce unable to find a way of stopping him.

He'd finally come unstuck the Saturday evening before last because some kid had moored a barrage balloon to a tree near an American bomber base and he'd flown straight into it. The base was Picton Hill. The kid was me.

Seven

I was off school for a month, but the minute the doctor said I was strong enough to leave my bed, wonderful things started happening to me, and I *will* bore you with the details.

First, a letter arrived. It was addressed to me, and it was from Air Marshall Sir E Leslie Gossage of RAF Balloon Command.

The Air Marshall thanked me officially for capturing the escaped balloon. The best bit of the letter said: *Your prompt and courageous action averted potential tragedy, and was instrumental in bringing down a cunning and a dangerous enemy.* Mum says she's framing it.

Next day I got another letter, this time from the Commanding Officer at Picton Hill. It was an invitation. The men at the base wanted to throw a party in my honour (they spelled it honor). I could bring as many kids as I liked as long as I also brought my mum, my sister and my bike. I'd no idea why I was to bring my bike, but as for Wendy, she was beside herself with joy. Seems she was in huge demand lately as the sister of the kid who'd messed up a much-feared foe. In a month I'd gone from an embarrassing nuisance in her life to the brother she couldn't do enough for. I wish you could've seen the sweets, the badges and aircraft-recognition manuals she carted home for me. They made me the most popular boy in Picton: the envy of all my chums.

That same day, a reporter from the *Picton Post* came to the house to interview me. He brought a photographer with him, and we all got in his car and drove out to where the Mustang had crashed. It was still there, ringed by a rope fence, with a Home Guard sentry. The sentry let us in and I was photographed leaning on a blade of the plane's buckled propeller, trying to look like Douglas Fairbanks.

The report and pictures were in that week's paper, and when the story was picked up by the nationals, I was in them too.

I didn't look a bit like Douglas Fairbanks, though Wendy reckoned I did.

The morning I went back to school I had to stand on the platform with my arm in a sling while the headmaster told everybody what a brave, resourceful lad I was. What a credit to my family, my school and my country. What a shining example to us all in these dark days. I tried to believe him but it just didn't feel like me, and I think that's how it might be with *real* heroes too – they don't realise at the time.

At breaktime I was surrounded by kids wanting me to sign the pictures they'd cut from the *Post*.

I've saved the best till last. The party.

It was on a Saturday, the first Saturday in October, and I took seventeen kids. I could have taken every child in the village but Mum said it seemed cheeky. They had it in the officers' club, which they'd trimmed with miles of tinsel and crepe paper. There was a real American Airforce band like Glenn Miller's, but playing stuff kids like. There were balloons (not

barrage balloons!) and paper hats. There were neatly wrapped presents of sweets and chocolate by everybody's plate, and all the airmen cheered and clapped as I

came in with Mum and Wendy and some of our neighbours. Oh, and my bike.

And the food. I don't know where they got it all but it covered three long tables and it wasn't spread out – it was piled up. We just stood gawping at it.

'I didn't know there was this much grub in *England*,' breathed Mum.

We ate, drank, danced, sang. We played games and we laughed. It started at five o'clock and went on till nine, when the trumpet player blew a long note to get everybody's attention and the Colonel mounted the platform.

And then came the best bit of all. An airman lifted my bike on to the stage and the Colonel produced some stencils and a little can of paint. He crouched over the bike and did something quick and deft with a brush, and when he straightened up there was one of those little swastikas fighter pilots paint on their planes to show how many enemies they've shot down, and beside the swastika, in crisp capitals, were the words, JOHNNY GOT A ZERO.

Glossary

Blackout (page 17)

It was illegal to show a light which might be seen from the air. No street lights.

Daylight raid (page 30)

Bomber-raid carried out in the daytime.

Iron Cross (page 37)

A German decoration for gallantry.

Land-girls (page 4)

Women recruited to work on farms, releasing males to join the military.

Mustang (page 43)

American fighter aircraft.

pinny (page 36)

A pinafore or apron.

salvage (page 11)

Materials for recycling: metals, paper, fabrics, glass.

Sten gun (page 17)

A submachine gun: British infantry standard issue.

VC (page 31)

Victoria Cross. Britain's highest gallantry award.

wireless (page 1)

Radio

wizard (page 2)

1940s equivalent of 'mega' or 'wicked'.

Zero (page 2)

The Mitsubishi Zero-Sen: Japan's best fighter aircraft.

If you enjoyed this
MAMMOTH READ try:

Hurricane Summer

Robert Swindells
Illustrated by *Kim Palmer*

It's World War Two and Jim has a fantastic
new friend – a fighter pilot.

Jim worships Cocky and looks forward to
his every visit.

But war has a way of changing people's
lives – and friendships may bring pain
as well as joy.